I Like to Read® books, created by award-winning picture book artists as well as talented newcomers, instill confidence and the joy of reading in new readers.

We want to hear every new reader say, "I like to read!"

———————————————————————————————————

Visit our website for flash cards, activities, and more about the series:
www.holidayhouse.com/ILiketoRead
#ILTR

This book has been officially leveled by using the F&P Text Level Gradient™ Leveling System.

1, 2, 3, Pull!

Emily Arnold McCully

I Like to Read®

HOLIDAY HOUSE • NEW YORK

"Can I be in your
show?" said Min.

"No," said Ann.

That night—

Snow
by Ann
and Bess

A tree fell.

"Oh, no!" said Ann.
"We can't have the show here."

Ann pushed.

"It is too big," Min said.

"We need a crane!" Min said.

She ran off.

The girls went to work.

"Look!" said Min.

"Look!" said Min.

"1, 2, 3, pull!"
said Ann and Bess.

"Push!" said Min.

"Now can I be in your show?"
said Min.

And she was!

For clever Liza and Annie

I LIKE TO READ is a registered trademark of Holiday House Publishing, Inc.

Copyright © 2021 by Emily Arnold McCully
All Rights Reserved
HOLIDAY HOUSE is registered in the U.S. Patent and Trademark Office.
Printed and bound in April 2021 at C&C Offset, Shenzhen, China.
The artwork was created with pen and ink and watercolor.
www.holidayhouse.com
First Edition
1 3 5 7 9 10 8 6 4 2

This book has been officially leveled by using the F&P Text Level Gradient™ Leveling System.

Library of Congress Cataloging-in-Publication Data
Names: McCully, Emily Arnold, author, illustrator.
Title: 1, 2, 3, Pull! / Emily Arnold McCully.
Description: First edition. | New York : Holiday House, [2020] | Series: I like to read
Summary: Min wants to be in Ann's show, and after building a crane to remove
the tree that has fallen on the stage, she gets her chance.
Identifiers: LCCN 2019015361 | ISBN 9780823445097 (hardcover)
Subjects: | CYAC: Creative ability—Fiction. | Cranes, derricks,
etc.—Fiction. | Performing arts—Fiction. | Elephants—Fiction.
Classification: LCC PZ7.M478415 Mg 2020 | DDC [E]—dc23
LC record available at https://lccn.loc.gov/2019015361

ISBN: 978-0-8234-4509-7 (hardcover)

ALSO BY **Emily Arnold McCully**